NOW LET ME FLY

The Story of a Slave Family

written and illustrated by DOLORES JOHNSON

Macmillan Publishing Company   New York
Maxwell Macmillan Canada   Toronto
Maxwell Macmillan International   New York   Oxford   Singapore   Sydney

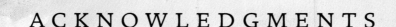

ACKNOWLEDGMENTS

In the fall of both 1990 and 1991, I was commissioned by the Children's Museum of San Diego, California, to write a story and create illustrations for an educational and cultural program called Roots & Wings. The Roots & Wings exhibits were mounted in 1991 and 1992 for Black History Month, and were funded solely and generously by the Ronald McDonald Children's Charities.

Roots & Wings is a collaboration between the museum and a small group of knowledgeable and accomplished women from the San Diego Chapter of Jack and Jill of America (an educational organization), who are dedicated to telling the African-American story to all children with complete honesty and sensitivity. Their names are Chris Mitchell, Felicia Shaw, Dayle Veasey, and Bea Kemp, and I humbly thank them.

I would like to acknowledge the assistance of the Children's Museum staff, particularly Bea Thurber, Director of Exhibits/Education, to whom I dedicate this book. Without Bea's support and guidance, I would never have been able to produce the exhibits and, subsequently, this book.

I would also like to thank Bart Thurber, Professor of English, University of San Diego, who provided invaluable help in the editing of the exhibit manuscripts.

Lastly, I would like to warmly thank Judith R. Whipple, my editor at Macmillan, who recognized my need to tell this story, and gave it wings.

Library of Congress Cataloging-in-Publication Data. Johnson, Dolores. Now let me fly : the story of a slave family / written and illustrated by Dolores Johnson. – 1st ed.   p.   cm. Summary: A fictionalized account of the life of Minna, kidnapped as a girl in Africa, as she endures the harsh life of a slave on a Southern plantation in the 1800s and tries to help her family survive. ISBN 0-02-747699-5 [1. Slavery—Fiction. 2. Afro-Americans—History—To 1863—Fiction.] I. Title. PZ7.J631635No 1993   [Fic]—dc20   92-33683

AUTHOR'S NOTE

From the mid-1500s to the mid-1800s, millions of African men, women, and children were taken forcibly from their homes and sold into slavery in the Americas. It is not known, even today, exactly how many millions died during the brutal capture, the forced march to the coast, or the agonizing voyage which brought them across the sea to this continent.

This book is a fictional account of one family's life in the constrictive grip of slavery. It is not a pleasant story, nor does it have a happy ending. Yet it is a story that must be told.

We all live with the legacy of slavery, even today. We must do all we can to insure that oppression of any group of people will never again be tolerated. We all are diminished when even one of us is not free.

I will never forget the day I first wanted to fly. My name was Minna then. I lived in Africa. It was many years ago, in 1815, but I can remember the day as if it were yesterday. My life was so happy then.

That day my mother and I were selling baskets and mats of straw at the marketplace. I became troubled when I saw a beautiful bird beating its wings against its wooden cage trying to escape. "You should be free, little bird," I whispered. I opened the cage door and watched as the bird spread its wings and flew away. I wished I could fly above the clouds with it.

My mother didn't scold me, even though the man who owned the bird shouted and waved his fists angrily at me. She just pressed some of our baskets into the man's hands to quiet him, and then said these words to me: "You did the right thing, my daughter. No living thing should ever be confined."

Later, as we crossed the savanna on our walk home, I heard the sound of drumbeats. "Mother!" I said in anticipation. "Do you hear the drums? Will there be dancing tonight or will the old ones tell their stories?"

"No, child. There is no joy in the sound of those drums," said my mother. "Hurry, we must get home."

When we arrived at our settlement, day had already dissolved into night. Many had gathered in a circle, their faces lit by the flickering campfire. The council of elders was meeting, presided over by my father, the chief. It seems a man from our compound named Dongo was on trial. I was not surprised, for this was not Dongo's first trial.

My father challenged Dongo. "It is said that you kidnapped some of our people and sold them as slaves. No one has seen you commit this outrage. But your past leads us to believe you are the only one among us who would harm us. Therefore, you are banished from this settlement, Dongo. Leave here and never come back, or your life will come to a quick and painful end."

Two men led Dongo away.

The next morning, as I played in my family's compound, I hummed the songs my mother sang to me as a baby. Only footsteps away, my mother ground grain with the other women while humming the same soft melodies of love and family.

When I thought I saw the little bird I had freed from its cage at the marketplace flying above me, I followed its flight all the way to the outskirts of the settlement. I flapped my arms as it flapped its wings, as if that could allow me to fly. Therefore, I didn't hear the footsteps that came up behind me. Nor did my mother hear my muffled screams as my kidnapper covered my mouth with his hand and dragged me away. All that could be heard echoing through the trees were Dongo's rantings: "Banish me, will you? Banish me?!"

I will never forget how it felt to be forced to walk, bound and beaten, for endless miles, each step taking me farther away from my mother and father. As I was marched, hundreds of other shackled and stumbling black men, women, and children,

taken as prisoners of war or kidnapped like me, joined us. We were herded by slave catchers like Dongo across Western Africa up to the edge of the western shore.

Within days, pale, ghostlike men arrived to transact business with Dongo and the others. The white men took us, a few at a time, in small wooden boats to a large ship anchored offshore. There they forced us to lie on rough wooden planks, side by side, so close together that there was no more than a whisper and a prayer between us.

What I will forever remember is meeting a boy named Amadi who sat beside me on the foul-smelling ship. Within moments of our meeting, he began to take care of me and I took care of him. When Amadi was sick with the dreaded fevers, I comforted him by singing the songs my mother taught me. When I tossed and turned with hunger, Amadi often said, "Take some of my gruel, little bird." As he wiped away my tears, Amadi would say, "Raise your head high, Minna. You are the daughter of a prince, the granddaughter of a great king. Yours is a great African heritage. No one can ever take that from you."

It was three long months before the big wooden ship finally dropped anchor on the shores of a land called America. They herded those of us who had survived the painful voyage off the ship in shackles and chains. Amadi and I stood on a platform in front of many white men and women who bid for us as though we were cattle or goats at the marketplace. A tall white man with the cold eyes of a snake bought Amadi and me for what I later found out was less than one hundred dollars each.

The man who bought us forced us to call him "Master Clemmons." Then he took away our names and told us, "Never speak a word of your savage language again!" Even though we were just children, Master Clemmons put Amadi and me to work in his cotton fields—from dawn to dusk, six days a week —until our backs nearly broke under the weight of our labor.

Almost overnight, Amadi and I grew from boy and girl to man and woman. As we grew, so did our love for one another. Soon our master gave us permission to get married. Every slave on the plantation came to watch us "jump the broom" into marriage at the wedding ceremony.

In time I gave birth to four beautiful children. Amadi and I raised our family in a tiny shack with the meager rations our master gave us and these rags on our backs as our reward. Though we lived in misery, captured in the cage of slavery, at least we had each other. But then I thought my life would truly end when my master told me, "I have sold your husband away."

It had been years since I'd heard my father's voice, and years since I'd felt my mother's caress. And then my husband was taken away before I could even say good-bye. I was never to hear another word from him again. My four children were all that I had in my life. I had to do all I could to try to keep the rest of my family together.

My hopes for my family were denied as soon as my oldest child, Joshua, began to grow toward manhood. By then everyone could see that my boy had a special gift. It's as if when he talked to the horses, they understood every word. Master Clemmons saw the bond my son had with animals and sought to profit from it.

The last time I ever saw Joshua he was in chains in the back of a wagon. He was on his way to be sold to another plantation, just as his father had been sold away only one year earlier.

"Please, Master, don't tear my family apart again. You can't sell Joshua. Don't sell my son!" I pleaded.

But Master Clemmons just pushed me aside. "That boy is more mine than yours!" he yelled as the wagon drove Joshua away.

Word was passed across country from slave to slave. After what seemed an unbearably long time, I found out that Joshua had been sent to the Randolph plantation, hundreds of miles away. Joshua will learn from their blacksmith all about the anvil and the fire. He will probably be hired out to bring more profits to his new master. A promise that Joshua made was also passed on to me. He vowed, "I will save every penny I am allowed to keep to buy freedom for my whole family."

My second child, Sally, was so smart, she taught herself to
read by listening to our master's children at their lessons.
But in Georgia it was against the law for a slave to know
how to read.

So Master Clemmons took a whip to my Sally. She just stood
there and took the lashing and did not even cry. That child has
a will of iron and a head that won't be bowed. I feared for her.
That's no way for a slave to be.

So I woke Sally one night, hugged her, and put her in the
arms of friends who would risk their lives taking my child up
North to freedom. I cry every time I hear the song they sang
when I saw her for the very last time. They were signaling to
the other escaping slaves to "Steal Away."

Months later I received a letter. I had
to find someone to read it to me. The moment
I first heard it, I memorized every word:

Mama,
*   Please don't worry about me. I am safe, though our*
travels were not easy. For six weeks we forded streams
and walked hundreds of miles at night, always
following the North Star. During the day, we
fell asleep in cold, wet, dark caves as we hid
from slave catchers. Free black people, and
sometimes even white people, offered us refuge.
*   Mama, you should have seen how happy*
we were when we arrived at the rock
with the "P" that told us we were at
the Mason-Dixon line. We knew that
in the state of Pennsylvania we could
finally be free!
*   I love you, Mama.*
*   Sally*

My boy Mason was smart like his sister and talented like his brother. He had a gift, but it wasn't how fast he could pick a row of cotton. That boy would take the banjo his daddy made and play it till even the birds tried to dance.

But my master saw the joy we found in Mason's music. He raised his whip to my boy to stop his banjo playing. And I knew right then that if Mason stayed on this plantation, he would only become a beaten, broken slave in the fields.

I sent word up North to Sally, the daughter I had not seen in six winters. In due time she answered my prayers. A strange black man came to our door and said, "I have come to help Mason 'steal away.'"

I waited six months to hear what had become of my son. Then I found this note slipped under my cabin door.

Mama,

Mason has been taken to Florida to live with a Seminole Indian family. For now, Mama, this is the best I can do to help Mason be free. Don't worry. Somehow I will find a way to bring our family back together again.

Your loving daughter, Sally

Katie is my last child. She is my youngest...my dearest Katie. I do not know what I will do if she is ever taken from me.

Katie is now working in the plantation's Big House. She has humbled herself to Master Clemmons's daughter. Our young mistress has told my daughter that neither she nor I will ever be sold if Katie remains her dutiful servant.

I am telling my last child the story of her heritage, the story my own parents once told to me. I am showing her how to make beautiful quilts and pottery from coils of red Georgia clay, like the ones I made as a child in Africa. We will probably never be released from this prison of slavery and rise to freedom like my Sally and my Mason. But Katie and I will somehow find comfort in our lives.

Katie and I often walk together up to the boundaries of the Clemmons plantation. As we walk, we hear singing, and if I try real hard, I almost hear my mother's voice. The women are singing the old hymn, "Now Let Me Fly," a song about a promised land that slaves can only find up in Heaven. But when I hear that old song, I search the sky for that little African bird, and I dream of freedom.

EPILOGUE

Minna and Amadi's children were forced to choose different paths to freedom. Over one hundred and fifty years later we can only try to imagine what might have happened to them had they really existed.

Despite the fact that he became a skilled blacksmith, Joshua, Minna and Amadi's oldest child, was never able to buy his family's freedom. Most slaves were unable to save the substantial funds necessary. Joshua raised a family of his own and passed his skills and knowledge down to his descendants.

Sally, like Sojourner Truth, spent her whole life speaking out against slavery and helping to bring hundreds of slaves out of bondage in the South.

Mason, like other fugitive slaves, made a new life in a Seminole Indian settlement in Florida. When the Seminoles were uprooted by the U.S. Government in 1842 and forcibly relocated to Oklahoma, he moved there as well with his new family and lived the remainder of his life as a Seminole brave.

Minna, Katie, and their descendants continued their brutal existence on the Clemmons plantation until the end of the Civil War some twenty years later, and the subsequent ratification of the 13th Amendment in December, 1865, which finally made all African-American men, women, and children free.